DEDICATION

This book is dedicated to my newest daughter, Elizabeth. Welcome to the family.